Swishy the Jellyfish

Written by Wang Yimei

Illustrated by Bai Wanwan

CARDINAL MEDIA

Swishy the jellyfish loved all the shapes and colors in her watery world. "Hey, there's a star!" Swishy said. "And that's a great circle. Ooh, what a wonderful shade of orange!"

But Swishy dreamed of visiting the land above water. "I wonder what orange looks like up there?"

One day, Swishy swam into a sandcastle a boy named Robbie was building. "I like your house," Swishy said.

Whoosh! A waved washed the sandcastle away.

Robbie laughed, "My real house is over there. Would you like to see it?"
"Yes, please!" Swishy said.

Swishy floated over a glove sitting on Robbie's table. "Ooh, this is a funny shape," she said.

Then Swishy dove into one of Robbie's shoes and said, "This looks a bit like a shell."

Robbie laughed, "My foot goes in that."

"This hat has a swishy shape
like you," Robbie said.
"That goes on my head,"
Robbie's mom said.
Swishy smiled.

Swishy saw lots of shapes
but she was still searching
for one special color.

"Can we go explore the town?"
Swishy asked.

"Yes!" said Robbie. "Let's go!"

Robbie bought some orange juice and shared a sip with Swishy. She was delighted. This was it! "Now I'm a wonderful shade of orange!" Swishy said.

Robbie and Swishy wandered all over the town. There were as many shapes and colors above land as in her watery world.

Soon it was time for Swishy to return to her ocean home. Robbie stood on the shore and waved, "Come back anytime!"

"See you soon!"
Swishy called out
as she splashed
back into the sea.

Swishy did visit Robbie many times. And they always had a wonderful adventure.

Text Copyright © Wang Yimei
Illustration Copyright © Bai Wanwan
Edited by Marie Kruegel
English Copyright © 2018 by Cardinal Media, LLC.

ISBN 978-1-64074-036-5

Through Phoenix Juvenile and Children's Publishing Ltd.
Printed in China

2 4 6 8 10 9 7 5 3 1